ANGELMOUSE

Missing Skates

by Rodney Peppé

One afternoon Angelmouse and Quilly were watching the falling snow.

"I'm glad I don't have to go out today," said Angelmouse, polishing his halo. "I hate getting snow on my thingamajig."

Suddenly, there was a knock at the door. As Quilly opened it, some snow and a message blew inside. But there was nobody there.

"It must be for you," he said, closing the door.

"I'm not reading it," said Angelmouse.

"I will, then," said Quilly, taking the message. "It says: **Oswald and Little Petal need help**."

"I don't care!" said Angelmouse. His halo began to wobble.
"I don't want my thingamajig freezing!"

"Come on!" said Quilly. "Or you won't have a thingamajig!"

They found Oswald and Little Petal by the pond.

"No skates! No skates!" said Oswald.

"Oswald said he'd teach me to skate," said Little Petal.

"But he's lost his skates, the dippy duck."

"They're probably buried in the snow," said Angelmouse.
Just then he saw someone who might be able to help!

"Hutchkin! You're good at digging," called out Angelmouse. "Could you help us?"

"I, like, dig digging, man," drawled Hutchkin.

"Ossie's skates are buried in the snow," said Angelmouse. "Can you find them?"

"I'll give you an extra big carrot from my shop, if you do, Hutchkin," added Little Petal.

Hutchkin began to burrow in the snow. He dug a lot of holes in no time at all. And then he found something!

"Hey, man," called Hutchkin. "Look!"

"My skates! My skates!" shouted Oswald, hopping up and down with joy.

Hutchkin began to pull something out of the hole.

"No, man," gasped Hutchkin. "It's like a monster frozen carrot! Wow, that's a meal and a half! I've got to get this home."

Oswald was very sad.

"What are we going to do now, Angelmouse?"
asked Little Petal.

Luckily, Angelmouse had an idea.

"There's Elliemum," he cried. "She can help us!"

Angelmouse asked Elliemum if she could use her trunk to blow away the snow. That way, explained Angelmouse, they could find Oswald's skates.

Elliemum agreed to do her best.

"Stand back please, everyone," she said.

She took a deep breath… and blew away the snow.

But there were no skates to be seen.

"No skates! No skates!" sighed Oswald.

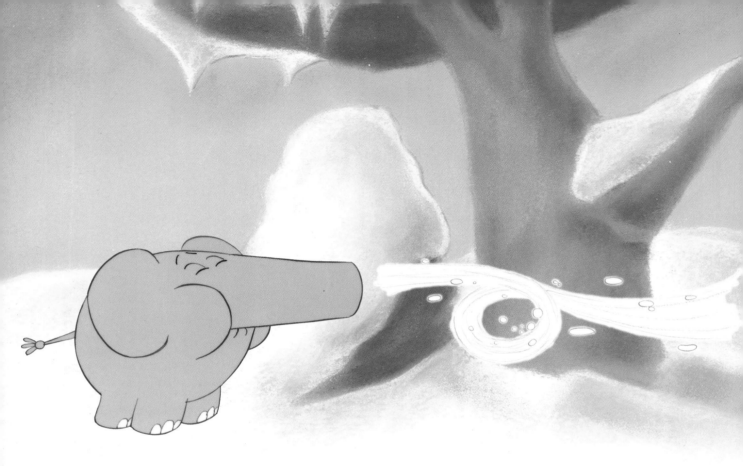

Baby Ellie wanted to help too.

"Blow! Blow!" burbled Baby Ellie.

"That's right, dear," said Elliemum, not giving up hope.

"Stand back, everyone. Baby Ellie wants to blow too!"

Baby Ellie blew just like Elliemum. Only, this time…

…poor Little Petal was in the way!

"Ow!" she cried, getting a face full of snow.

"I'm sorry, Little Petal," said Elliemum. "That was very careless of you, Baby Ellie!"

But just then, Baby Ellie gave a huge sneeze. And once more Little Petal was covered in snow.

By now it was getting dark.

"No skates! No skates!" Oswald reminded everyone.

"I don't think Angelmouse can help anymore, Oswald," said Quilly.

"Yes, I can, Quilly," said Angelmouse. "I've had an idea!
We're going to the Pole star. The coldest star of all."

At long last, they reached the Pole star.

"It's freezing!" chattered Quilly.

"Now, we need to see the Winter Angel," said Angelmouse. "I think he lives in that ice palace."

They knocked on the door.

"Hello, we're looking for the Winter Angel," said Angelmouse.

"That's me," said the angel. "I've been expecting you. I've got some things for you, Angelmouse."

The Winter Angel handed Angelmouse
a pair of tiny skates.

"One pair of skates. Size – doll, small," he said.

And then he gave Angelmouse a bigger pair of skates.

"One pair of skates with 'go-faster' stripes. Size –
duck, medium."

The Winter Angel gave Angelmouse another package.

"What is it?" asked Angelmouse.

"A halo cosy," explained the Winter Angel.

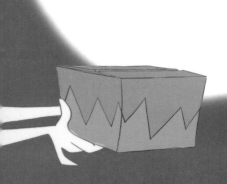

"To keep my thingamajig warm?" asked Angelmouse.

"Exactly," replied the Winter Angel.

"Thank you!" said Angelmouse. "Thank you very much!"

"Goodnight!" said the Winter Angel. "And safe journey."

Angelmouse and Quilly flew away into the night.
As they set off for home, they heard the Winter Angel call,
"Goodbye! And don't drop the skates!"

Oswald and Little Petal were waiting for them.
Angelmouse gave them their new angel skates.
"Cool skates! Cool skates!" said Oswald.
"You're an angel, Angelmouse!" said Little Petal.

So Oswald and Little Petal went skating after all, thanks to Angelmouse. And Angelmouse loved his halo cosy. It kept his thingamajig wonderfully warm!